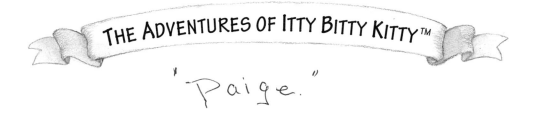

THE ADVENTURES OF ITTY BITTY KITTY™

"Paige."

Library of Congress Cataloging-in-Publication Data
Keeshan, Robert
Itty Bitty Kitty makes a big splash / by Bob Keeshan ; illustrations by Jane Maday
p.   cm.
Sequel to: Itty Bitty Kitty.
Summary: While enjoying her new home at the hotel, Itty Bitty Kitty has a scary
adventure at the pool and a narrow escape from the manager, the only staff
member who does not like her.
ISBN 1-57749-018-5
1. Cats—Juvenile fiction. [1. Cats—Fiction. 2. Swimming pools—Fiction.
3. Hotels, motels, etc.—Fiction.] I. Maday, Jane, ill. II. Title.
PZ10.3.K246It 1997
[E]—dc20   96-30521

First printing
Printed in Singapore

02 01 00 99 98   7 6 5 4 3 2 1

For a current catalog of Fairview Press titles,
please call this toll-free number: 1-800-544-8207.

Produced by Mega-Books, Inc.
Design and art direction by Nutshell Design, Inc.

Publisher's Note: Fairview Press publishes books and other materials related to
the subjects of family and social issues. Its publications, including *Itty Bitty Kitty
Makes a Big Splash,* do not necessarily reflect the philosophy of
Fairview Hospital and Healthcare Services or their treatment programs.

Itty Bitty Kitty
Makes a Big Splash

by Bob Keeshan
illustrations by Jane Maday

Fairview Press
Minneapolis, Minnesota

Itty Bitty Kitty loved her new home. She hardly remembered where she had lived before, but she did remember the woods where she had gotten lost in a terrible thunderstorm. And she especially remembered being chased by a hungry red fox. Luckily, Itty Bitty Kitty had escaped the fox and found shelter in a big hotel tucked away in the woods.

She quickly became the pet
of all the employees in the
hotel — the bellhops, the
doormen,

the desk clerks,
the cooks,

the waitresses, the
housekeeping staff —

everyone but Mr. Dunhoffer, the manager. He was not fond
of cats, and he certainly did not want one in his hotel.

The guests didn't mind having a kitten around. It made the hotel feel more like home. And the hotel workers became very good at keeping an eye out for Mr. Dunhoffer.

Once in a while he would catch a glimpse of Itty Bitty Kitty out of the corner of his eye. But before he could make sure he had really seen what he thought he had seen, someone would distract him with a question to answer or a problem to solve.

Itty Bitty Kitty was a very curious kitten. She also liked to keep busy. That was partly why she liked the hotel so much. Not only were there lots of places to explore, but there were also many interesting things to do. She could help the housekeeping staff clean the rooms.

She could entertain the guests at wedding parties.

She could give advice at business meetings.

She was even willing to assist the chef — but he didn't really seem to want her help.

Itty Bitty Kitty tried new things every day, but she particularly liked escorting the guests through the revolving front door, which was a lot like a merry-go-round. One afternoon while she was helping the doorman, a girl about eight years old came in. When she saw Itty Bitty Kitty, she scooped the kitten up in her arms.

"What a cute kitty! Are you staying here, too?"

Meow, said Itty Bitty Kitty.

"Good," said the girl. "My name is Heather. Let's go back to my room and you can meet my little brother."

Heather skipped down the hallway, cradling Itty Bitty Kitty in her arms. When they got to the room, the kitten crawled up on her shoulder while Heather unlocked the door.

"Look what I found," she said to her brother. "Isn't she cute?"

"You said you'd take me to the pool," Michael complained. "How can we go if you've got a cat?"

"Don't worry," said Heather. "I'll just wrap her up in a big towel and she can come with us. We'll go to the indoor pool so she can't get lost outside."

Itty Bitty Kitty had never been to a pool before. What would it be like?

At the pool, the children put the kitten on their small raft and gave her a ride. Itty Bitty Kitty didn't know what to make of so much water in one place. The bouncing of the raft was a bit scary, but interesting, too. Curious, she sat still and looked around.

A shrill whistle caught their attention. "Hey, kids, get that raft out of the pool!" the lifeguard called. "It's against the rules."

Heather and Michael pushed the raft to the side of the pool. While Heather lifted out the towel and the kitten, Michael slid the raft onto the tiles.

"She'll be safe here," Heather said, placing Itty Bitty Kitty next to a lounge chair. Then she went back into the water to play with her brother.

The kitten watched as Michael did the dog paddle and Heather stood on her hands in the shallow end of the pool.

The children played for a little while longer, then Michael said, "I'm hungry."

"Okay," Heather said. "Let's go. Mom and Dad should be back from their meeting by now."

They climbed out of the water and walked over to the chair. No kitten.

"She's gone!" said Michael. "Where did she go?"

"I don't know," said Heather, "but I hope she's all right."

It was almost dinnertime, and the other swimmers left the
pool soon after Heather and Michael. The lifeguard picked
up her whistle and left, too.

In the far corner, sharpening her claws on a potted palm,
was Itty Bitty Kitty. She glanced at the pool and saw the
raft, still resting at its side. Would it feel the same way on
the ground as it did in the water?

The small kitten raced over and jumped on. The raft skidded across the wet tiles and over the edge of the pool. Itty Bitty Kitty was floating on the water all by herself! This was new!

She crept to the side of the bouncy raft and stared down into the water. She saw ripples and all kinds of reflections. And there was another kitten staring back at her! She hissed and swatted at the water with her paw.

Whoops! The raft flipped over and dumped Itty Bitty Kitty right into the pool. She had never been underwater before. This was one new experience she didn't like. What had she gotten herself into?

Frightened, she thrashed about, trying to get out from beneath the raft. With a great effort, she pushed forward and was free. Since cats can swim, Itty Bitty Kitty could stay afloat even though she was in over her head.

Itty Bitty Kitty paddled toward the edge of the pool. Just then the door opened and a great booming voice echoed through the room.

"Where is that lifeguard?" Mr. Dunhoffer bellowed.

Justin, one of the bellhops who had befriended Itty Bitty Kitty, heard him from the lobby and came in. "Susan's gone home for the day, Mr. Dunhoffer."

"I don't believe it!" stormed the manager. "Not only is there a raft in my pool, there's a cat in there, too. I want it out! Now!"

Justin hurried to the edge of the pool where Itty Bitty Kitty was struggling up the steps. He scooped her out of the water, but kittens are good at wriggling free when they don't want to be held, and Itty Bitty Kitty was wet and slippery. She squirmed out of his grasp and made a dash for the door.

"You left the door open!" shouted Mr. Dunhoffer. "The cat's getting away! Catch it!" The manager started to run along the side of the pool, but the tiles were still wet, and he slipped. With a huge *splash!* he plunged into the water, clothes and all.

"Aargh!" he sputtered. "Get me out of here!"

Justin held out a hand to help his boss from the pool. "Gee, Mr. Dunhoffer," he said, trying to hide a grin, "didn't you see the sign, NO RUNNING IN THE POOL AREA?"

"Not another word, Justin! Just get me out of here!"

Meanwhile, Itty Bitty Kitty found her way to Heather and Michael's room. She meowed as loudly as she could and scratched on the door.

Heather opened the door to a shivering and very bedraggled
kitten. Her mother gave her a towel, and the little girl dried
Itty Bitty Kitty off and put her to bed. There Itty Bitty Kitty
stayed while the children went off to dinner and a movie with
their parents.

When Heather and Michael got back, Itty Bitty Kitty was curled up right where they had left her. They offered her a bit of food they had brought back, but for once, Itty Bitty Kitty wasn't even curious. She was much too sleepy after her adventure and her narrow escape from Mr. Dunhoffer.

The children quickly put on their pajamas and snuggled into bed, one on each side of Itty Bitty Kitty. Lulled by the contented purr of the tiny kitten, they soon fell fast asleep.